Gillian _____ writing child _____ books _____
fifteen _____ She w _____ the Carnegie _____ her
novel Wolf _____ and wa _____ runner-up for _____ ard
with A Map of Nowhere. The Great _____ se
won _____ the Whitbread Children's N _____ ar
the Smarties Book Prize. She is also th _____ or c
Walker young fiction title, _Posh Watson_ _____ arried
four children, her hobbies include or _____ teering
playing the piano.

Arthur Robins has illustrated several children's books,
including the Walker titles _Impo, Little Rabbit Foo
Foo, I _____ w an Old Lady_ and _The Finger-eater._

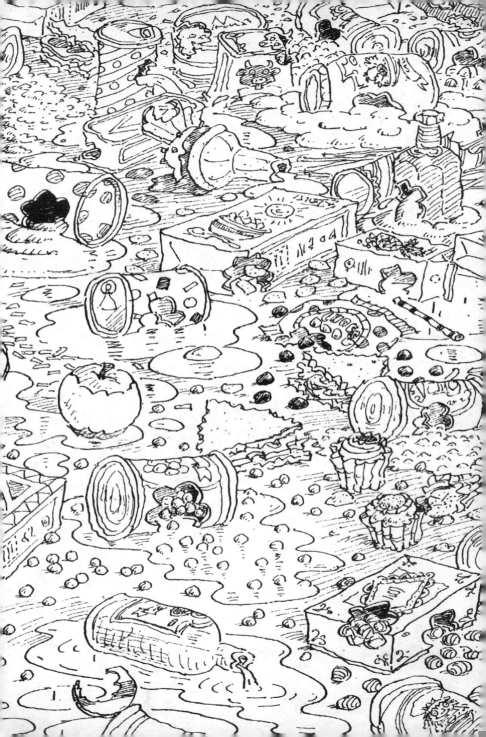

Some other titles

Art, You're Magic!
by Sam McBratney

Holly and the Skyboard
by Ian Whybrow

Jolly Roger
by Colin McNaughton

Little Luis and the Bad Bandit
by Ann Jungman

Millie Morgan, Pirate
by Margaret Ryan

Pappy Mashy
by Kathy Henderson

The Snow Maze
by Jan Mark

Tillie McGillie's Fantastical Chair
by Vivian French

The Unknown Planet
by Jean Ure

GILLIAN CROSS

Beware OLGA!

Illustrations by Arthur Robins

WALKER BOOKS
AND SUBSIDIARIES
LONDON · BOSTON · SYDNEY

First published 1993 by Walker Books Ltd
87 Vauxhall Walk, London SE11 5HJ

This edition published 1994

4 6 8 10 9 7 5

Text © 1993 Gillian Cross
Illustrations © 1993 Arthur Robins

Printed in England

British Library Cataloguing in Publication Data
A catalogue record for this book is
available from the British Library.

ISBN 0-7445-3188-8

CONTENTS

OUTSIDES ARE HORRIBLE!

Fiona hated crusts. And skin and
peel and all the tough, chewy
outsides of things. But people never
stopped nagging her about them.

"Eat your apple peel," said her mother. "It'll give you rosy cheeks."

Fiona cut off the peel and hung it on the washing line for the birds.

"Don't leave your potato jackets!" her father said. "They'll make your eyes sparkle."

Fiona screwed them up and shot them through the window with her catapult.

"Finish your crusts," said her grandmother.

Fiona hid the crusts in her pocket
and took them down the garden to
feed the hedgehog.

No one could make her eat the outside of anything. Until the day she went down to the baker's to buy the bread on her own.

It was nearly closing time. She roller-skated all the way down the hill and straight into the shop.

"A large brown loaf and three doughnuts, please," Fiona said.

"Yes, *ma'am!*" The baker put them into her backpack and smiled at her.

The baker leaned over the
counter to look at her more closely.

Everyone knows
the crust's the
best part. It
makes your hair
curl.

I don't want
curly hair!

"Crusts are horrible," said Fiona.
"So is rice pudding skin. And apple
peel. And everything that comes on
the outside of food. I hate outsides."

"Do you now?" said the baker.
"Well, fancy that. Maybe I ought to
send my friend Olga to see you.
She *loves* outsides."
And he stood in the
shop doorway,
watching Fiona
thoughtfully
as she skated
back up the hill.

OLGA COMES TO TEA

The next day, just before tea, Fiona
was in the garden, making a dam.
She saw a reflection in the pond
and looked up.

There stood a strange girl, exactly as tall as Fiona, but quite different. Her teeth gleamed, her cheeks were rosy and her hair stuck out in corkscrew curls.

Fiona blinked. "Well – er –"

Before Fiona could get any
further, Olga was at the back door,
waiting to be let in.

Fiona opened the door and called,
"Mum!"

Her mother yelled back, from
upstairs. "I'm busy. Your tea's on
the table."

"Tea!" said Olga.

She was through the door and
into the dining-room. When Fiona
caught up with her, she was gazing
at the table.

She snatched up a cheese
sandwich and

all the crust was gone. Grinning,
she flicked the sandwich across the
table on to Fiona's plate and picked
up another one.

Fiona started to eat the sandwich,
but she was only halfway through
when Olga tossed her the second one.

And then another and another. In
ten minutes there was nothing left.
Not even a crust.

Fiona swallowed her last
mouthful and looked at the table.

Olga looked at the warm milk and her eyes gleamed. "Skin!" She grabbed the mug and hooked the skin off with her long, pink tongue. Then she passed the milk back to Fiona.

"Fantastic!" Fiona took the milk and looked hopefully at the blancmange. "Could you...?"

Olga smiled.

The blancmange skin vanished.

Fiona grinned. "This is really good!" and she took a huge spoonful of blancmange.

Before she could swallow it, Olga turned to the cakes. "Outsides for me, insides for you. OK?"

Fiona's mouth was full of blancmange. She wanted to stop Olga, but she couldn't get the words out quickly enough.

Before Fiona could speak, Olga ate all the icing and left the plain cakes.

"That's not fair," Fiona said.

Olga tossed her curls. "Yes, it is. You don't like outsides."

"I like *icing*."

"Icing is *outside*. Icing makes your fingernails shine. What's next?"

Olga looked round and saw the fruit bowl on the sideboard.

Before Fiona could stop her, she had eaten all the apple peel. And the banana skins.

Fiona stared at the bananas for a moment, feeling rather peculiar. Then she grabbed the fruit bowl and pushed it into the sideboard, to save the grapes. When she turned round, the room was empty, and there were strange slurping noises coming from the kitchen.

Olga was sitting on the floor by the fridge, licking cream off the trifle and eating the outside of the sausage rolls.

"Stop!" Fiona grabbed Olga's shoulder and tried to drag her away, but it was impossible. She was as solid as a rock. Olga grinned and grabbed three yogurt cartons out of the fridge.

Olga bit into the plastic carton, chewing it up like a biscuit. The yogurt dribbled down her chin and ran all over the floor.

Olga licked her lips.
And reached for a milk bottle.

HELP!

Fiona ran into the hall and grabbed
her skateboard. There was only one
thing to do. A second later she was
whizzing down the hill towards the
baker's shop.

She zoomed in at the door,
bumped into an old lady buying
a cream cake, and went sailing
up in the air.

She landed behind the counter
and the baker looked down at her.

"Olga?"

"Yes!" wailed Fiona. "How do I
get rid of her?"

"Hmm. We'll have to see about
that." The baker pulled the end off
a loaf and began to chew it. Then
he pulled off another bit and held it
out to Fiona.

He looked at her.

She took the crust and bit into it
and the baker smiled.

"But she won't!"

The baker smiled again. He reached under the counter and pulled out a piece of paper.

Pineapple upside-down cake,
it said. Chewing her crust, Fiona
trudged back up the hill, reading
the piece of paper as she went.

She pushed open the kitchen
door and…

Wheee-bam!

She slipped on a raw egg white, skidded across the floor and landed in a puddle of baked beans.

Olga was eating the tins!

There were big bites out of the jamjars too. And the cornflakes

packet. And the orange squash bottles. And the sugar bags. The things from *inside* were scattered everywhere.

And Olga was grinning.

Fiona forced herself to grin back.
But she didn't waste any time. She
grabbed a bowl and started to
scoop things up – flour and butter

and sugar. Eggs and milk and
golden syrup.

And pineapple rings.

Olga watched suspiciously.
"What are you doing?"

"Making a *delicious* pudding,"
said Fiona.

Olga licked her lips. "Insides for you, outsides for me?"

"All right." Fiona smiled cunningly. "Could you fetch some spoons? They're in the sideboard. Next to the grapes."

"Grapes!" Olga's eyes gleamed and she was off...

Quick as a flash, Fiona poured
the golden syrup into a glass dish
and dropped in the pineapple rings,

spooned the cake mixture on top
and pushed the dish into the
microwave.

Then she peeped into the dining-room. Olga was busy eating grape skins.

Fiona smiled.

The moment the upside-down cake was cooked, she took it out of the microwave. The sponge outside was set, and through the glass she could see the inside – delicious, sticky pineapple.

Running a knife round the edge
of the sponge, she put a plate
over the dish and turned the whole
thing over.

The sponge fell on to the plate
with the pineapple on top and the
sticky pineapple juice running
down the sides.

The sponge outside was inside and the pineapple inside was outside.

Fiona looked towards the dining-room door.

UPSIDE-DOWN CAKE

There was Olga, at the table, with a spoon in her hand. As Fiona put the pudding on the table, she stared at it, licking her lips with her long, pink tongue. Then –

the pineapple vanished and only the
plain sponge was left. Olga pushed
the pudding across to Fiona.

"You can have that," said Olga.

Fiona took a deep breath. "I don't like outsides," she said.

"*Outsides?*" Olga looked down at the remains of the pudding and turned pale. "*What was that?*"

Pineapple upside-down cake.

Olga stared for a moment and
then she shrieked.

Her hair shot out all over her head in long, straight spikes. Her rosy cheeks turned green and her

neat, white teeth cracked from top to bottom. She jumped to her feet and pointed her finger at Fiona.

Quick as a flash, Fiona snatched up a sausage roll with all the outside gone.

Olga gave a loud, terrible wail
and towered up, taller and taller
and thinner and thinner until –

There was a flash of light and a puff of thick, black smoke. Olga vanished – and a whirlwind hit the kitchen.

Tins appeared from nowhere and
baked beans jumped back into
them. Milk slurped into bottles and
cornflakes rattled into packets.
Eggshells flew through the air and
snapped together, and cream
squirted itself, in
swirls, on
to the
trifle.

In ten seconds, the kitchen was back to normal. Fiona looked round and grinned. Then she got up and walked into the dining-room.

The fruit bowl was standing on the sideboard. The apples had their peel back, and so did the bananas. And each grape had its own, unbroken skin.

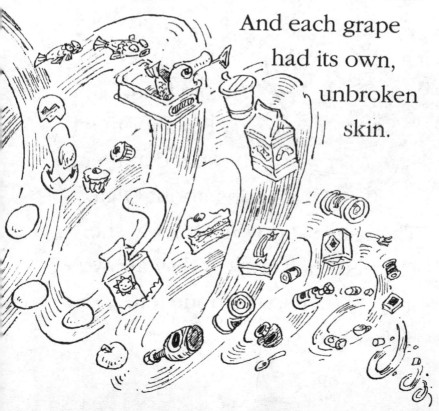

Thank goodness! thought Fiona. *Everything's come back!* Then she remembered something and she turned round to look at the table.

All the crusts from her sandwiches had come back too. There they were, piled up in a big heap.

For a moment she stared at them, thinking about Olga. Then she sat down. Quickly she chewed each crust and swallowed it, until there were none left.

Just in case.

From that day on Fiona ate every crust she was given. Blancmange skin, too. *And* apple peel. *And* every other skin and rind and peel. She wasn't taking any risks.

Her cheeks grew rosy and her eyes sparkled, her teeth gleamed and her fingernails shone. And her hair was beautifully…

(Even grown-ups
don't know everything.)

MORE WALKER SPRINTERS
For You to Enjoy